Robert Brogan was destined to be sheriff in the small town of Pride, Oregon. He moved to Pride when he was eight after his mother's mysterious disappearance. Always following the rules and sticking up for the weak, he had only one thing in mind after graduation—tracking down his mother. But after almost ten years of looking with no luck, he makes his way back to his hometown. When tragedy strikes, he's given the opportunity of a lifetime. Being sheriff in the small town of Pride gives him the chance to pursue the girl he just can't keep his mind off.

Amelia Blake can never forget the boy that saved her from certain danger ten years ago. When she comes home after her father's death, she only plans on a short visit, but her mother's failing health and her feelings for Robert persuade her to move back home. When sparks fly, she can't help finding herself falling fast for the new sheriff in town.

Table of Contents

Other titles by Jill Sanders

The Pride Series
Finding Pride – Pride Series #1
Discovering Pride – Pride Series #2
Returning Pride – Pride Series #3
Lasting Pride – Pride Series #4
Serving Pride – Prequel to Pride Series #5
Red Hot Christmas – A Pride Christmas #6
My Sweet Valentine – Pride Series #7

The Secret Series
Secret Seduction – Secret Series #1
Secret Pleasure – Secret Series #2
Secret Guardian – Secret Series #3
Secret Passions – Secret Series #4
Secret Identity – Secret Series #5
Secret Sauce – Secret Series #6

The West Series
Loving Lauren – West Series #1
Taming Alex – West Series #2
Holding Haley – West Series #3

Jill Sanders

Serving Pride

Jill Sanders

SERVING PRIDE

Follow the Pride Series and Jill Sanders online at:
Web: www.jillmsanders.com
Twitter: jillmsanders
Facebook: jillmsanders

ISBN: 9781301061136
Copyright © 2013 Jill Sanders
Edited by Erica Ellis
http://www.ericaellisfreelance.com

Dedication

To my editor...

*I can't thank you enough,
for making my books read as
well as they do in my head.*

Jill Sanders

Chapter One

Little Robert listened to his mom crying in the next room. He knew that he couldn't go in there yet. He had to wait until Roy left before he could go see how bad the damage was from the fight. Chances were Roy would either pass out drunk within fifteen minutes or he'd grab his keys and leave, heading down to the local bar to get even more wasted.

It was a hell of a way to spend his eighth birthday. He had enjoyed the party earlier; all of his friends had attended and he'd gotten loads of cool presents. But shortly after the last guest had left, Roy had started drinking. It had taken less than an hour for his mother to do or say something that had caused the fight. Robert knew it wasn't her fault.

He could remember a time when his mother had been pretty and strong. Back when his real father, Robert Sr., had been alive, she'd smiled and laughed a lot. But when he was six, his dad had died in a car accident and his mother stopped living.

She hadn't started dating until just last year, and the first person she'd picked was Roy. She'd met him at the bar where she worked six nights a week. At first Roy had smiled and brought presents for them. Shortly after he moved in to their small two-bedroom apartment, the fights began. Robert didn't know why his mother kept him around, why she allowed him to still live there. There really wasn't anything the man was good for. After all, shortly before he'd moved in, he'd lost his job at the steel mill.

Robert didn't like him not only because of this, but also because the man called him Robby, which he couldn't stand. He always used a tone, like he was making fun of him or that he had a secret joke somehow tied up in his nickname. But his mother acted like she loved him, and so Robert had tolerated him.

Plus, Roy had promised them both that he'd find a new job and take care of them. But then he'd started drinking. Robert even thought that he was using drugs, though he couldn't really tell. He never took drugs in front of him, but Robert had listened carefully to the police officer who had talked to his class when his school had a drug awareness week. The man had spoken about saying no to drugs, but hadn't really talked about how to tell if someone else was on drugs.

After the officer's planned speech was done, Robert had walked up to him and asked him how to tell if someone else was on drugs. The man had looked at him funny, and then he sat down and talked to him, giving Robert a few things he should look out for. He asked Robert if he was okay and tried to get him to tell him who Robert thought was on drugs. But Robert didn't want to get Roy, or worse, his mother, in any trouble, so he'd just told the man that there were some kids that bugged him on his walk home.

He'd enjoyed talking to the officer and had eyed the man's gun like it was candy. He knew guns were dangerous and needed to be handled by professionals, but man, he really wanted to see how much it weighed and feel how it felt in his hands. Maybe someday he'd get to hold a real gun and even fire it.

Now he listened to Roy leave, then waited a few more minutes before he crawled out of his bed with his Spider-man comforter and sheets. As he tip-toed down the short hall, he listened for the front door, just in case Roy decided to come back. If he did, Robert would make a bolt for his room. Roy had never hit him, probably because if he ever laid a hand on him, his mama will the man. She'd said so on many occasions.

"Mama?" He pushed the door opened and looked into the dark room. He could just make out his mother on the bed in the dark room.

"Go back to bed, honey." He heard her sniffle and she quickly rolled over, putting her back to him.

He walked over to the other side of the bed and looked at her. "Mama, are you okay? Should I call the police?"

"No, honey. We just had a fight. Roy's just stressed that he hasn't found a job yet."

"Mama, did he hit you?" Robert had been asleep for the first part of the fight. All the sugar and running around during his party had worn him out. He'd actually gone to bed an hour earlier than normal.

"No, baby. He just yelled." His mother sat up and turned on the light. Robert saw that her eyes were swollen red from crying. She still had on the dress that she'd worn for his party. It was her happy dress, as Robert liked to think of it. The pale yellow reminded him of better times with his father, for some reason.

She patted the mattress next to her and he climbed up next to her on the bed. When she wrapped her arm around him, he felt comforted. He loved the way his mother smelled, as fresh as a field of daisies. That's what his father had always said, and Robert had always agreed with him.

"I'm sorry to wake you. Did you have fun today?"

Being the eight-year-old boy that he was, he fell for the change of subject his mother provided and proceeded to talk for a few minutes about his party and all the cool presents he'd gotten that day. He fell asleep again, there in her arms, and she carried him back to his room and sung to him as she laid him back in his Spider-man bed.

The next morning when he woke, she was gone. There was no note, no goodbyes, nothing. Roy had come back and had fallen asleep on the couch, face down. When Robert tried to wake him, he'd just turned over and put the pillow over his head.

Robert thought that maybe his mom had gone to the store, so he got ready for school. He made his own lunch and grabbed a few slices of bread and some cheese for breakfast. Roy didn't move, even though Robert was being very loud in the kitchen.

When he left to walk for school, his mother still wasn't there. Leaving the apartment complex, he saw by his mother's car still parked in the parking lot, and for a second, he wanted to run back in the apartment to see if maybe she had just been hiding from him. She couldn't have gone anywhere without her car. He thought that maybe she'd taken Roy's truck, but when he looked, he saw that it was parked out back behind the apartments.

It took him twice as long as usual to walk to school that day, because he was so occupied by his thoughts. When he finally did make it to class, he was fifteen minutes late and received his third tardy that year.

Walking home with a note that needed to be signed, he stepped in to find Roy still on the couch face down. He'd forgotten to check and see if his mother's car was there, but he knew instantly that she wasn't home. She was supposed to work until midnight that night since she'd taken off the day before for his birthday party.

Walking into his room, he dumped his bag on his bed and got to work on his homework. He had an agreement with his mom. If he kept his grades above C's he would get to play Xbox after dinner. Since his mother was at work, he could eat dinner as early as he wanted, which meant more time playing games.

That whole evening, Roy didn't move. He'd walked by him several times to make sure he was still breathing and was slightly disappointed when he heard the man snoring.

The next morning, he rushed into his mom's room to find it empty. Roy was no longer on the couch. When he got home from school, neither of them were there. Since it was Friday, he called for pizza delivery and paid out of the money his mom hid for him. He spent the weekend playing video games and eating junk food.

When he went into school on Monday, he still hadn't heard from either his mom or Roy. Instead of going to his class, he'd walked into the principal's office and sat out by the receptionist. He told the older woman he needed to speak with Mr. Kent, man to man, before classes.

Finally, a few minutes later, Mr. Kent walked out and nodded to him to follow him into his office.

"Well, Mr. Brogan, what can I help you with today?"

Robert sat in the large leather chair and looked across at the principal.

"Well sir, I think something happened to my mom and Roy."

Instantly the man's face showed concern. "What do you mean?"

"I haven't seen my mom since last week and Roy took off, too. It's not like my mom to leave this long. Her work called and left a message, saying she was fired. Roy, well, Roy doesn't work and his truck has been gone for a few days."

"Who's been watching you?"

"No one, sir. I've been on my own since the day after my birthday." Robert hadn't realized tears were escaping his eyes and when a fat drop landed on his hand, he jumped and looked down at it like it had fallen from out of nowhere.

Mr. Kent picked up his phone, "Mary, can you call Child Protective Services, please. Tell them it's an emergency."

Robert can't really remember what took place in the days that followed, but less than a week later, he was on a plane to someplace called Oregon. He was going to live with his great-aunt by the ocean. He'd never seen the ocean and the excitement almost won out over the fear.

When they told him that they thought his mother had abandoned him, he screamed and kicked until they finally agreed that maybe something had happened to her. They hadn't found Roy or his mother's car or Roy's truck. Since he'd never known Roy's last name, something young kids don't think of remembering, and since the man wasn't on the lease, they didn't even know where to start looking.

Stepping off the plane, the first thing he noticed was that it was cold. New Mexico was always warm. Then he saw snow on the ground and his fear turned into excitement.

There was an older woman sitting in a wheel chair with a handmade sign that had his name on it in bright red and blue letters. Red and blue were his favorite colors. He saw this as a good sign.

Walking up to her, he dropped the hand of the stewardess who'd accompanied him on his flight. "I'm Robert Brogan. Are you my aunt Daisy?"

She leaned over and smiled at him. "Yes, sir, I am. I'd recognize you anywhere. You look just like your daddy."

The drive from the Portland airport to the town of Pride seemed to take forever. He didn't quite know what to say to his aunt. He found her car totally fascinating, though. He found her car totally fascinating She had it fitted with special controls so she could use her hands to work the gas and brake pedals. At first he'd been afraid of how she was going to get in the car. He'd wanted to ask if she needed any help, but she'd quickly hopped into her seat like she was a professional. What took her the longest was getting her wheelchair folded up and put in the seat behind her. He could have helped, but he was afraid he'd upset her.

"Well, Robert, I don't know what they told you, but I was your father's aunt. We were very close when he was younger, but when he moved down south, I guess we lost track of each other. I hadn't heard any news about him until he passed away." She looked over at him as she drove. "I hope you don't mind cats. I have a few of them. They make me feel better. I bet you're dying to ask me what happened to my legs, huh?"

He nodded his head in agreement and she laughed. She looked younger when she laughed and he couldn't help but smile back at her.

"Well, a while back, I had a stroke, and since then, my legs just won't follow what my brain tells them to do. Don't worry, the rest of me seems to be working just fine and since the doctor started giving me some new medicine, I've never felt better." She smiled at him again.

"Let's see, you're in the second grade?"

He nodded his head in agreement, again.

"Good, I think I've gotten everything set up for you to start school next week. I hope it's okay that I decided to let you have the rest of this week off. I don't think you'll miss that much. Besides, we'll have fun getting to know each other."

"I'm just staying here until my mom comes back." He wanted to shout it. He'd told the CPS worker over and over again that he wanted to stay at home. He was sure that his mom was going to come home and if he wasn't there, he was worried she would think that something bad had happened to him.

"It's okay, honey, we'll wait for her together. I'm sure she'll come back for you. You can just stay with me until she does. Will that be okay?"

This was the first person who'd actually believed him about his mother. Hearing her words made him finally believe that his mother wasn't coming back, that she couldn't come back for him, and he had a sinking feeling he knew why.

Chapter Two

Ten years later

$\mathcal{R}$obert left the school for the last time. Graduation was tonight and he couldn't wait to leave Pride tomorrow. He'd lived here ten long years, waiting for someone he knew would never return. It was time for him to leave and see the world. Maybe he'd head south to try and pick up his mother's trail. Or better yet, Roy's trail. The man must be out there somewhere.

Walking out, he spotted two jocks, Kevin and Ricky. They had their backs to him and he knew they were up to no good. He could hear the laughing and name calling from across the parking lot. Without thinking about it, he started walking towards them. He'd grown bigger and taller than the two football quarterbacks two years ago and had, on more occasions than he could remember, stepped in to save some poor kid from their wrath.

"Hey, why don't you guys go pick on someone...."

At that moment Kevin stepped back and Robert finally got a look at who they were bullying. His mouth went dry and he almost lost his footing.

Amelia Blake was the one girl he just couldn't be around. Every time he was, he reverted to a stuttering fool. She was a year younger than him, and he'd had a crush on her since the first time he saw her, on his first day of school in Pride. Her bright red hair and freckles had been so unique, he'd instantly liked her. He'd never seen anyone with such bright hair before. She'd been teased all throughout school, until sometime in junior high. She'd shown up on the first day of school after summer break and her bright red hair had darkened to a deep amber, her freckles had disappeared, leaving smooth porcelain skin, and everything else on her had matured as well. She had been beautiful before, but now, she was just stunning. His infatuation with her had tripled.

"What do you want mister goody two-shoes? Can't you see we want to be left alone with Amy?"

They had her pinned against the chain link fence that bordered the school parking lot. Her back was up against the fence, and he could see the fear in her green eyes. Her books were pressed against her beautiful chest, and he thought he actually saw a tear leave her face.

"Kevin, Ricky, don't you have somewhere else you're supposed to be?" He took a step closer, trying to show that he wasn't going to back down. After all, he knew he could take Kevin; he'd done it once already, just last year. Ricky, on the other hand, he wasn't so sure about, especially since there were two of them. What he needed was to level the playing field. Looking around the parking lot, he found that almost every car was gone, already.

"Leave us alone, twerp. We were just having fun with Amy. Weren't we? Tell him, Amy, we weren't doing anything wrong." Kevin's hand reached out and ran down her cheek. Robert watched as she flinched away. When Kevin reached to grab her, Robert stepped over and stopped his hand. Without thinking about it, he flung Kevin away from Amelia and watched as Kevin landed a few feet away.

Then he was being attacked from behind as Ricky punched his kidneys. He felt the blows, and before he could block them, he felt something snap. He turned and caught the third blow with his hand and easily blocked the next.

Amelia screamed and tried to move farther away. He got in a few good hits before he hit the ground, and the two started kicking him. Then he heard his buddy Todd Jordan's voice as he started running towards them.

When Robert looked up, he saw Kevin and Ricky driving away in Ricky's truck. Then Todd and his brother Iian were standing over him.

"Man, are you okay, Robert?" Iian asked. The kid was tall for the age of eight. Todd was in the same grade as Robert and had been his good friend since he'd arrived in town.

"Yeah." He sat up and tried to get his breath. Then he looked over at Amelia. She was still standing up against the fence, her books held tightly against her chest.

When he stood, she watched his every movement like she was in shock.

"Are you okay?" He got up and walked towards her with his hands out. He could feel every place where Kevin and Ricky's feet and fists had connected.

She nodded her head, and he saw a few more tears form in her green eyes.

"They—" she took a deep breath. "They wanted me to get in the car with them. They told me it was about time they initiated me into the Honeymoon pact."

Robert felt like running after those two. The Honeymoon pact was a pact the football team had to sleep with all the attractive girls in the school, whether they wanted it or not. In short, he'd just saved her from being abducted and raped by two jerks.

"You're okay. They're gone now."

Todd walked over to him. "Are you okay? You're lip is bleeding."

He wiped his mouth with his sleeve. "Yeah, they hit like girls." They all laughed and he started feeling a little light headed. The next thing he knew, he was on the ground with Amelia looking down at him. His head was in her lap and she was stroking his hair. He thought he could just lay there forever, looking up into her face.

"Don't move. Todd went to get Dr. Stevens," she said as she ran her fingers through his hair.

"Why would I want to move?" He thought he saw her smile, but then he felt a new pain, one that was so sharp, it left him gasping for breath.

"It's okay, you're going to be okay. You saved me, you know." His eyes had closed on the pain, but now he opened them to see more tears in her eyes. They ran down her face and dropped onto his shirt.

He tried to reach up and wipe them away, but when he moved his arm, the sharp pain was back.

Damn! Ricky must have broken his rib.

"Don't cry. They aren't worth it."

"I'm not crying over them, you fool. I'm crying because you're hurt and it's all my fault." She looked a little mad and he wanted to laugh.

"It's not your fault. I've been trying to find a reason to kick their butts for a while now."

She laughed again and looked up. "Dr. Stevens is here. If I don't get time to tell you later…" She leaned down and placed a soft kiss on his lips. He could taste her tears, and for a second he thought he smelled flowers. "Thank you for rescuing me."

Robert didn't make it to his graduation that evening. Instead he spent the night in the hospital with a broken rib and a punctured lung. He'd heard that both Ricky and Kevin had missed graduation, as well. They'd spent the night in a cell down at the sheriff's office. Considering that the sheriff was Amelia's father, they were lucky they were allowed to bail out the next day.

Of course when Robert arrived home to his aunt's place, she had a large gathering of friends who all praised him as a hero. He was okay with it since Amelia was there. Her mother hugged and kissed him while tears had fallen down her face, and her father had shaken his hand like he owed him everything.

Amelia watched Robert as he sat across from her. She'd never really paid much attention to him in school. He'd been one of those kids that had always stood in the back of the class pictures and was never really called out from the crowd. But after seeing him fight off the two boys, she had a new interest in him. While he had been passed out, and after Todd and Iian left to go get the doctor, she'd had plenty of time to look at him.

His eyebrows were dark and his eyelashes were long. His skin looked smooth and when she'd run her fingers over his face, she'd enjoyed the small stubble on his jaw. His hair was dark and thick and she'd liked running her hands through it. He was built like one of the fighters her dad watched on television every Saturday night, which made her wonder what he looked like without his shirt on. Would he have the same rippled muscles that most boxers had?

When his eyes had opened, she'd gotten lost in the dark chocolate pools.

How had she not noticed him before? What was she going to do to make him think she wasn't some fool who couldn't take care of herself?

Her face heated as she remembered feeling helpless and afraid. She felt a shiver run down her back at the memory of Kevin's hands on her. They had cornered her, and before Robert stopped them, they had both grabbed her chest and had pinched her until she almost cried.

Looking over at Robert, she wondered what his hands would feel like on her. She watched as he got up and made his way towards her. He held his sides a little and she could see him cringe slightly from the pain.

"Can I sit here?" He nodded towards the side of the couch her mother had just left. When she nodded, he slowly sat down.

"Are you okay?"

"Yeah, it only hurts when I laugh." He smiled at her.

"Well, I'll make sure not to tell you any jokes." She liked seeing his eyes spark when he smiled at her. "What are your plans now that you've graduated?"

He looked across the room at his aunt. His aunt, Daisy, had been confined to a wheel chair for as long as Amelia could remember.

"Well, I was actually planning to leave tomorrow. I'm heading south for a while. But with this," he motioned to his side, "I may be delayed a few days."

"South?"

"New Mexico. It's where I'm from."

"What will you do there?"

He looked at her and she thought she saw sadness in his eyes.

"I haven't figured that out yet. I just know that I have to get away from here for a while. Maybe I'll travel for a while, you know, see the world."

It sounded wonderful to Amelia. She had one more year of school, then her father and mother had already planned for her to attend college in Portland, close enough that they could keep an eye on her. Which wasn't too bad; after all, she loved her parents. But being able to travel and see the world sounded wonderful.

"Well, I hope you'll look me up when you get back."

He smiled at her and reached for her hand. "Don't let those guys corner you again. Promise me you'll be careful."

She nodded her head and wished more than anything that they were alone in the room. She wanted to feel his lips on hers again. Ever since she'd kissed them, she'd imagined doing it again.

Jill Sanders

Chapter Three

Ten years later

Robert's car almost stalled as he pulled into Pride. The thing was on its last leg and he'd been lucky to get this far. When he pulled up in front of O'Neil's Grocery on Main, he realized he was glad to be home.

As he parked, people turned their heads and looked to see who had just driven into town. He sat behind the wheel for almost a minute before he stepped out. When he did, the greetings immediately started. First the old men outside the barber shop yelled over to him. Then it was Mary and Betty, who had been walking into the grocery store. They both rushed over to give him hugs, then talked his ear off for over ten minutes. He finally pulled himself away from the pair and made it into the store to purchase some fresh flowers to give his aunt. He just couldn't see himself going home empty-handed. Not after everything she'd done for him.

It took almost another half an hour to get out the doors with the small bouquet in his hands. He knew that word traveled fast in town and thought that the news of him coming home might actually reach his aunt before he had a chance to step foot on her doorstep.

He was happy to see her sitting on the front porch, waiting for him.

"Betty called." She smiled up at him.

"Of course she did." He kissed her cheek and handed her the flowers as a tear fell down her cheek. She'd aged a lot in the time he'd been gone. So much so that he started to feel guilty for being gone so long.

It took him a week to get back into the swing of things. Since leaving, he'd done exactly what he'd planned. First he'd gone to New Mexico to try and track down his mother and Roy. After almost five years of working with the police there and coming up with a bunch of dead ends, he'd moved on and traveled for a while. A few years later he'd received a call from the Nevada police saying they'd found his mother's car, so he'd rushed across the country.

But instead of finding a trail to his mother, he'd found Roy.

The car had been abandoned in a parking lot at a casino. When he'd tracked down the security footage, he'd seen the frail old man on the video and immediately known it was Roy.

Roy's trail lead him from casino to casino. Tracking him had given Robert so much satisfaction, almost like he was on a hunt. The closer he got, the more energy he felt.

But then the trail had gotten cold and he'd headed back home. In all his time traveling, he'd studied. While in New Mexico he'd killed his time taking police courses, and to make money, he'd ended up working on the force. But his entire focus had been finding his mother.

Being a cop had just come naturally, so the first thing he did on the Monday morning after he returned to Pride was walk into the sheriff's office and apply for a job. He was greeted and hired on the spot. Evidently several of the deputies had moved out of town and they were extremely shorthanded. He and Sheriff Blake were the only two working there besides Stacy, the clerk and dispatcher.

He didn't want to feel like he was burdening his aunt, so he rented the apartment above O'Neil's Groceries. The small apartment was already furnished and it was in town, so he could easily keep an eye on everything.

Pride wasn't such a big place that there was a lot going on. Most of his calls were simple complaint calls. High school kids would get into trouble, sneaking into places they shouldn't. Or husbands and wives would argue too loudly and there would be a domestic dispute call. They also dealt with accidents on the main highway between Pride and Edgeview, a larger town just fifteen minutes away.

Some days he would end up patrolling the beach, but with winter coming there would be far fewer people visiting. He also helped the rangers patrol the state park. Kids like to party up at the overlook on Friday nights, and he'd swing by there to make sure nothing too crazy was going down.

He was only in his second month on the job when things took a turn. He was sitting at the small diner off the highway with the sheriff, when David grabbed his chest right there over his lunch and fell over.

Robert did CPR on him until Dr. Stevens arrived, then they took him away in the ambulance. Robert called Mrs. Blake and stopped by to pick her up and drive her to the Edgeview hospital. She'd been losing her sight since earlier that year and didn't drive. By the time they got to the hospital, David was gone.

Robert sat there with Mrs. Blake crying on his shoulder and wondered what he was supposed to do now.

Amelia was at work in Portland when she got her mother's call. It took her less than ten minutes to leave the small veterinary clinic. Packing while your eyes are flowing with tears was very difficult. She asked her neighbor to watch her place while she was gone, packed up Oscar, her five-year-old Siamese cat, and headed home.

While she drove she kept thinking of her father. She'd spent her entire vacation in Pride over the recent holidays. She remembered him smiling and laughing, and he'd looked healthy enough. She knew that he'd had more stress in the last year since his two deputies had quit and moved out of state. Her mother's deteriorating health had also caused him some stress. She just couldn't wrap her mind around the fact that he was gone. When she finally drove up to her parents' house a few hours after leaving Portland, it hit her.

The driveway was packed with cars and she knew the well-wishers were already there. There was a group of older women in town who saw to it that anyone who was going through a tough time, wouldn't be alone. Which usually involved a lot of food and people. Parking her car behind her dad's cruiser, she started to walk in when she heard a noise behind her. There was a group of older women in town who saw to it that no one who was going through a tough time in Pride would be alone.

Their plans usually involved a lot of food and people. Parking her car behind her dad's cruiser, she started to walk into the house when she heard a noise behind her.

She turned around and saw him standing against a tree trunk next to the cruiser. She recognized him immediately. Robert Brogan had been on her mind a lot over the years. Because of him, she'd had the courage to do things she never would have. She'd taken a year off and had traveled to places she'd wanted to see her whole life. Rome, Paris, Hawaii, and Australia had been the first on her long list. Then she'd settled back down and finished college. Being a veterinarian was something she'd dreamed of ever since she'd found a hurt bird and nursed it back to health when she was a child.

She'd also learned from her experience with Ricky and Kevin that day so many years ago and had taken nine years of judo. No one would ever corner her like that again.

She walked over to Robert, stopping just a few feet away.

"Are you going to come in?" He stood in the shadows and continued to just look at her.

"In a minute. I'm sorry about your dad."

She knew she must look a wreck. She hadn't even changed out of her scrubs and lab coat. Her eyes were probably all puffy and red from the tears that had flown down her face on the drive down here.

He looked the same, from what she could see. It was almost too dark in the shade of the tree to see his face clearly. His dark hair was cut shorter and his eyes were darker than she remembered.

"Thank you. I didn't know you were back in town."

"I've been back for over two months." He stepped forward, and she noticed that he was wearing a uniform much like the one her dad had always worn, but his shirt stretched tight over muscles she didn't remember him having the last time she'd seen him. His arms and chest were wide and she realized she'd been wrong; he *had* changed, a lot. His eyes showed a deepness that she hadn't seen before. He seemed taller and more powerful than the boy she remembered.

"I hear you're a veterinarian now. Your dad was always talking about how proud he was of you."

She could feel the tears building. She knew she was stalling, putting off going into the house so she could avoid the realization that he wasn't there.

Robert must have noticed, because he walked forward and engulfed her in his arms. It was nothing more than a brotherly hug, but it did wonders for settling her heart.

She didn't realize she was crying until he said, "Shh, it's okay. You can get it all out." He ran his hands into her hair and held her to his chest.

He was practically a stranger and here she was blabbering all over him. Why did he always have to see her when she was the most vulnerable? His arms were wrapped tightly around her, one of his hands at the back of her head, holding her close to his chest. She could feel that she'd gotten his shirt wet with her tears and felt stupid that she'd soaked it.

Leaning away, she looked into his eyes and could see that none of it mattered. He was looking at her with kind eyes and had a slight smile on his lips. She'd dreamed of kissing those lips so many times over the years.

Taking a step back, she used her hands to wipe the tears from her face.

"I'm sorry. I lost it for a minute."

"You don't have to apologize. I can only imagine what you're going through." They stood there in silence, watching each other for a few seconds. Finally, he grabbed her hand and started walking her towards the house. "I'm sure your mother is going to be happy to see you. There are so many people in your house. I needed to step out and get some fresh air. Everyone is going to be glad that you're home."

When she entered the house everyone stopped and looked at them. She didn't even register that he was still holding her hand. Then she saw her mother sitting on the couch and rushed over to engulf her in a hug.

After the funeral two days later, the house was packed once again. Amelia was dressed in her simple black dress pants and a black sweater and was thankful it hadn't rained that day; the weather had held for the simple ceremony. The whole county had shown up for her father's funeral.

He'd been sheriff for as long as she could remember, over thirty years of service. He had been set to retire in three years. Her parents had planned for their retirement her whole life. They had taken family vacations when she was a child, but had only driven up or down the west coast. Once, they had traveled to Yellowstone National Park, but that was as far as her mother would allow them to go.

Maybe that was why she'd had such a huge desire to travel after high school. She felt like her parents were content to live their lives in Pride and had no real desire to ever leave.

Not that she didn't like Pride. After all, it was home. She knew everyone in town and felt warm and comfortable here. But she had wanted to see the world in her youth.

After her travels, she'd had a better understanding of why her parents had picked Pride as a place to live. People here were generally good. You could really count on them in a time of need, and for the most part, everyone helped everyone else out.

Her mother had yet to be left alone since Amelia had arrived home. Her friends all stayed with her and made sure her needs were taken care of, which made Amelia think about her own future. She knew her mother had lost most of her sight over the last five years. She was looking frailer than she had in the past, and Amelia just couldn't imagine her living in the house alone.

By the end of the day she knew that she needed to move back home to care for her. For now she was surrounded by the whole town, but once things settled down, there was no way her mother could live without someone here.

Within three weeks she'd closed up her life in Portland. She'd called and given her employer her notice the day after her father's funeral. She'd also called her landlord and told him she'd be moving out at the end of the month. She was breaking her lease, but due to the dire circumstances, he'd waived all the fees.

Now, as she drove in front of the small moving van back to Pride, she wondered what the next few years would hold for her. She knew she could ask Tammy, the head veterinarian at the local clinic, for a job. Hopefully, there was an opening. If not, she could always find something else to do. After all, living with her mother, she wouldn't be hurting financially.

Her dad had had life insurance and since the house had been paid off in the seventies, her mother's bills were quite low. As for her, she still had car payments she had to make and two credit cards she needed to pay off, but that was all.

Her mother had been so excited when she'd told her she was moving back, she'd told everyone she could. Since her eyesight had started to fail, she'd hardly left the house. Her mother had really relied on her father to take care of her. He'd done all the shopping, but she'd still done all the cooking and cleaning around the house. She may not have been able to see very well, but she could still fight dust and make a mean meat loaf.

When Amelia pulled into the driveway, she noticed the cruiser was back. Quickly checking her reflection in the mirror, she cringed at the image that stared back at her. Her red hair had frizzed and was falling out of the bandana she'd tied it up with. She hadn't worn any makeup that day, because she'd spent her entire morning packing and loading boxes.

She fixed her hair quickly and hoped she didn't look too ragged in her faded jeans and oversized sweatshirt. She stepped out of her car and watched the movers pull into her mother's drive. She motioned for them to back into the garage where she would store all her stuff until she decided what she was going to do.

Looking back to the house, she saw her mother and Robert walk out the front door. He had a smile on his face as he helped her mother to the chair on the deck. She walked over to them and couldn't help but smile when she noticed the new badge on his lapel.

"Hello, Sheriff Brogan."

He nodded and smiled. "They made it official this afternoon. I can't believe they trust me to run this town, at least temporarily until election time. Then I'll have to run officially."

"Well, of course they made him sheriff," Her mother chimed in. "You deserve it, too. After all, you saved our Amelia from the thugs back in school." Leave it to her mother to bring that up again. After that incident, her parents had idolized him. She'd heard so often what a great young man Robert was, she'd almost gotten sick of it. Almost.

Her dad had always told her that she needed to find someone like him to settle down with. She supposed when Robert moved back into town, her dad had jumped at the chance to make him a deputy. That's probably how he'd gotten the job, anyway.

Looking at him now, she realized he did look mighty fine in the uniform.

Jill Sanders

Chapter Four

Robert couldn't stop smiling at Amelia. He watched her boss the moving men around like they were her minions. She looked very sexy in her torn jeans and faded sweatshirt. He kept telling himself he should leave, but just couldn't seem to pull himself away.

He'd stopped by originally because he wanted Mrs. Blake to find out from him personally that he'd been voted by the city council to take over for her husband. He thought it best to tell her himself and had asked the board members not to call her. He knew some of the town women had quietly, and disappointingly, put down their phones.

He'd been nervous driving over here, not knowing how she'd take it. But she'd hugged him and told him how proud she was. Then, Amelia had driven up and he'd found another reason to stay. Looking at her was a delight.

As he sat on her mother's porch and watched her coordinate the movers, he remembered being pleased when he'd first moved back into town and had found out that she was unmarried. He knew she lived out of town, but hearing from her father how her life had turned out had been wonderful. David had always been proud of his little girl and he had shown it every day that they had worked together.

"You know, David and I always hoped you would come back into town. We knew that your aunt has missed you since you left."

He looked at the older woman and remembered that she and his aunt had been very close. Since his aunt's last stroke, she hadn't been able to drive. One of her friends, Martha, had moved in and taken care of her, which was one of the main reasons he'd quickly moved into the apartment above the store.

"I know my aunt is happy that I'm staying. It just tickles her to think that I'm sheriff now. Her words, not mine," he said as she laughed.

An hour later, as he walked into his apartment for the night, he couldn't get Amelia out of his mind, the way she'd smiled at him, the way she walked, and how she smelled of flowers.

He'd always known he was attracted to her. Hell, he had been for years. But he hadn't expected the pull of desire he'd had when she'd smiled at him tonight.

His new job was going to be a lot more demanding and he knew he needed to focus. He still had two deputies to hire, not a small task in a town of eighteen hundred people, especially with the budget the town council had given him.

Tossing his belt off, he took his service weapon and put it in the small safe he had installed the day he'd gotten the job. His own 9 mm sat in there as well. He'd been fascinated with weapons, ever since he was a young child, and he enjoyed carrying his gun around. He could remember his father showing him his service weapon. He'd been a policeman on the force in New Mexico, and Robert wondered if that's what had called him to the force.

Whatever it was, he wasn't about to give it up. He had every intention of running for sheriff next year. He had even started looking for a house of his own. He couldn't stay in the small apartment for much longer. He would never really have any privacy with Patty O'Neil downstairs.

By the end of the next day he was seriously questioning his sanity, as the small town was flooded with reporters from all over the world.

George and Iian Jordan were missing somewhere off the coast of Oregon. They'd left yesterday for Iian's birthday sail and had gotten into trouble. The last message from them had been received earlier that day when they'd relayed a distress call to the coast guard.

George Jordan was head of Jordan Shipping, a large international company, so of course reporters from all over had gotten a hold of the story and flocked to the small town.

Since Robert hadn't had time to hire anyone yet, he'd quickly called in two school friends to help him take care of the growing crowd that was hell bent on disobeying his orders.

He shook his head as he noticed a few cars were double parked on Main Street, blocking traffic. After getting them to move, he made sure to block off the small road leading to the Jordan house so the rest of the family could have some privacy.

When he swung by the Golden Oar, the family's restaurant, he noticed it had been closed for the day. That didn't stop a few reporters from trying to camp out there. Since it was private property, he told them to move on.

But for the most part, everyone spent the day waiting down at the docks, knowing the first word of what was happening would be from there.

Later that next evening, he received a call from the office that Iian had been found alive and had been flown by helicopter to the hospital in Edgeview. The search for Mr. Jordan had been called off due to bad weather.

Robert stood in front of a group of reporters and relayed the information. They had all shouted questions after his statement, none of which he knew the answers to.

Finally, after leaving there, he went into Edgeview to see if there was anything he could do for the family. Todd had been in the same grade as him in school and had always been a close friend.

When he arrived, he saw Amelia hugging Lacey, Todd and Iian's sister. Todd's wife, Sara, was sitting next to Amelia, looking very pale. He'd forgotten how small Lacey was. Her short dark hair made her look even more petite next to Amelia's vibrant, long red tresses. He wondered how Amelia had made it there so quickly.

When he approached, the three of them looked up. "How is he?"

Amelia answered, "He's banged up. He hasn't woken yet, but they say he's going to make it. He has a mild case of hypothermia and quite a concussion, not to mention a few broken ribs."

Lacey just sat there, staring off into space. He felt bad for her so he sat next to her and took her hand in his. It was so much smaller, almost childlike.

"Lacey, if there is anything I can do, just let me know." She nodded her head and a tear slipped down her cheek.

He looked up in time to see Todd walking across the room towards them.

"Has he woken yet?" Lacey asked, eagerly jumping up from the chair. When Todd shook his head no, she slumped back. Sara stood and walked over to hug Todd quickly. Robert stood as Todd walked over and shook his hand. "Thanks for handling all the press."

Robert looked at him questioningly.

"You were all over the news here." Todd motioned towards the television set and sure enough, Robert could see his own face on the screen as the news station replayed his statement.

"I only wish they'd leave. It's my second official day on the job and I haven't even made it into the office yet. I'm sorry they called off the search for your dad temporarily."

"If he was still alive, he would have been with Iian." Todd looked at Lacey, and Robert could tell they had both accepted the fact that their father was gone.

Just then a few more townspeople rushed in and headed towards the family.

"If you want to be alone, I can corral everyone out of here." He asked Todd.

"No, it'll be good for us, I think." He pulled his sister up and into a hug. "We'll deal with this, with our family by our side."

He sat down next to Amelia and looked at her. He noticed the short black skirt she was wearing. The tight silver shirt hadn't escaped his notice either. Her hair was curled and pulled up so that small ringlets dropped down around her face. How could he not be distracted with how she looked? "How did you get here so fast?"

"I was visiting Lacey at the restaurant and decided to come along for support. Lacey and I used to be really close in school." She turned and looked at him. "Actually, I drove her car over here since she was too upset to drive. When you leave, if you can give me a ride back home…?"

"Sure, as long as you don't mind riding in the back." She smiled at him.

She'd thought he was joking, but as she sat in the back of the cruiser she couldn't help but laugh.

"Are you really going to make me sit back here the entire trip back to Pride?"

He smiled at her in the mirror. "It's the law."

"When did you get so picky about following the rules?"

He smiled at her. "Besides, this way you can't distract me."

"Distract you? Has anyone ever told you the seat back here is sticky?"

"It's the cleaner I use to disinfect them. I had Kevin Williams back there last week." He watched her eyes sharpen.

"Is he still causing problems?"

"He's gotten a lot worse. He and Ricky are regulars down at the station. I guess they were always heading towards trouble."

"Well, I'm glad I haven't seen either of them since I left Pride eight years ago. Tell me about yourself, Robert. What have you been doing since you left Pride?"

She had been dying to ask him that since the last time she'd seen him. So far she'd heard a few details at the grocery store, but no one really seemed to know what he'd done other than work as a cop in New Mexico. She wondered if he had traveled like he'd told her he wanted to.

"Well, I left here and tried to find my mom in New Mexico. I worked so closely with the police, I just sort of fell into becoming one. Then I did some traveling for a few years. I went to Europe, China, and even Africa." She saw his brows crinkled in thought. "But, I came back to the States and then came home."

"What brought you back?"

"I suppose I was just tired of not having a home. Besides, when I talked to my aunt, she sounded a lot worse and I thought it was time I came back to be with her. She's the only family I have."

"Robert? What really brought you back to the States?"

He took a deep breath and she could tell he was fighting something. "They found my mom's car. Roy had abandoned it in Vegas. I actually got my hopes up that maybe I'd finally track her down. But I guess I've been fooling myself into thinking she was still alive."

They pulled into the empty parking lot at the Golden Oar and stopped by her car. She watched as he got out and opened the back door for her. She got out and closed the car door, trying not to notice how close he stood to her. She leaned back on the car and pulled her jacket tighter around her, blocking out the cold wind coming from the ocean. The parking lot was dark and she couldn't help thinking how good he looked in his uniform jacket.

"I'm sorry about your mother." It came out as a whisper. He'd moved even closer to her and she was finding it harder to breath.

"Amelia, what would you do if I kissed you right now?"

She smiled and reached for the front of his jacket to pull him the rest of the way towards her. When their lips met, she could have sworn her toes curled. His hands were on her hips, holding her close. She could feel his heat radiating from his body and leaned even farther against him, wrapping her arms around his narrow waist.

"Mmm, you taste just like you look." He pulled back and looked into her eyes as she felt the chill biting into her legs. The skirt was stylish, but the stockings were doing little to keep her warm from the chill. "I know it's too cold out here to do this for much longer, but I just have to have another quick taste."

He bent his head and after the kiss ended, she no longer felt the chill.

"I have next Monday off," he said as he walked her to the car. "I was hoping that you'd like to go somewhere with me?"

She smiled. "As long as I don't have to ride in the back again." He chuckled.

"No, this time we'll take my personal car. How about I pick you up around seven?" When she nodded, he leaned down and kissed her again.

"Mmm, I could do this all night, but I know how chilly it is out here. Go get in your car before I decide to follow you home and finish this." He smiled down at her and then started to walk away.

"Robert?" She waited until he turned back towards her. "Thanks."

"For what?"

"The ride home and the kiss. I'll see you on Monday." She got into her car and looked back at

Robert's car in her rear-view mirror. She laughed when she saw him fist pump the air.

Jill Sanders

Chapter Five

It took a few days for everything to finally die down in town. Once the coast guard had officially called off the search for George Jordan, most of the reporters had quickly left. There were still several camped out in Edgeview Hospital, waiting for news of Iian who had yet to wake.

Robert had found some time to hire two deputies. One was a young cop from Edgeview and another an older gentlemen from another small town half an hour away. Both had experience in law enforcement.

He settled into his paperwork and his job and felt like everything was finally slipping into a pattern. There had been quite a few parties around town lately to keep him busy. It seemed the high school kids had decided to have a week long party that hopped from house to house. He didn't mind staying busy, since it had kept his mind occupied through the week. He didn't know why, but he was actually nervous for this date.

He'd dated plenty over the years, but had never been in a steady relationship. It seemed every time he started getting serious, he ended up pulling out of the relationship. He knew why, too. He had a date with her tomorrow night.

Amelia waited by the front door, feeling like a teenager again.

"You look lovely, dear," her mother said from across the room.

"Thank you, Mom." She said skeptically. It was hard to trust her mother's opinion, since she probably couldn't even see her clearly.

"Don't pull that tone with me, young lady. I may not be able to see you clearly, but there's nothing wrong with my hearing. Besides, I know what my daughter looks like, and you always look lovely." Amelia walked over to her mother and gave her in a light hug.

"I'm sorry, mom. I'm just a little nervous."

"I remember when your father came to pick me up for our first date. Your grandpa gave him the evil eye and tried to scare him off, but David just stood there and took it all with a smile." Her mother laughed and still managed to look a little sad at the same time. "Thirty-five years with that man and I wish I had thirty-five more."

"Mom, do you want me to stay with you tonight?"

"Oh, heaven's no. You go out with Robert, have fun. After all, it's what your father would have wanted. He always liked that young man. Especially since he came back to town. He had always hoped that you and he would get together."

"I know. It's funny how one little event could sway you both so quickly."

"Little event? We owe that young man a lot. I believe he saved you that day. Beside, Ricky and Kevin have done nothing but get in trouble since they were born. Their parents never really gave them much attention. What they needed was a good —" She was interrupted when there was a slight knock on the door. "Oh, here he is now. You two go off, have fun. Don't worry about me. Betty was going to swing by later tonight and play some gin." Amelia bent down and kissed her mother's cheek.

"Night, mother. I'll see you when I get home."

"There's no rush now, go and have some fun."

When Amelia opened the front door, she was greeted with a bunch of daisies. When Robert moved them down to peer over them, his smile faltered and she was satisfied that she'd worn the right dress.

He looked very sexy in a gray button-up shirt with dark colored pants. His leather jacket made him look dangerous, something she knew she'd never thought about him before.

"You look beautiful." He handed her the flowers and smiled even more.

He just couldn't get over the hot red dress she was wearing. The fact that it was skin tight didn't escape his notice, nor did the low back and the plunging neckline. Hell, anyone with eyes would easily be on fire around her. He felt the heat just from sitting in the same car as he drove towards Edgeview. Since the Golden Oar was still closed, the nearest nice restaurant was fifteen minutes away.

He didn't know if he'd make it through dinner with her and keep his eyes from popping out of their sockets. He tried to get his mind off her body and talked to her about anything he could think of.

He listened to her stories about how she'd traveled after school, and how she'd gotten her job in Portland. He knew most of it already from her father, but hearing her tell it was more interesting. He couldn't get over how much she'd changed. She used to be very shy and had always been quite the introvert, but now, listening to her, she sounded very courageous and outgoing.

"You've changed a lot since the last time I saw you," he said over dinner. They were seated at a little place right along the beach. The dim lights and soft music added to the atmosphere. It was just what he'd wanted.

"Really?" She smiled at this and for a second he thought she had a secret she was hiding from him.

"Yes." He leaned over and grabbed her hand across the table. He liked seeing the spark in her eyes when he touched her. "You seem more courageous. More..." He didn't have the words.

"It might have something to do with the fact that I've taken Judo since the last time you saw me. After what happened, I wanted to make sure I could protect myself."

"Wow, Judo?" He smiled as he thought about it, and he found himself getting more turned on by her. In New Mexico he'd trained in Judo and Tae Kwon Do, as well as attending a few boxing classes. He'd also had some gun classes that he had to stay up with. It had seemed at times that he spent more time attending classes than searching for his mother.

"What do you plan on doing now that you're home?" he asked on the way back to town. He hating thinking that the evening was coming to an end and tried to drive as slowly as he could.

"Well, I've applied for a job at the veterinary clinic in town. Hopefully I will get it. After that, I hadn't really thought about it. How about you?"

"I've decided to run for sheriff next year. I've been looking at a few houses around town to purchase."

"Really? Which houses?"

"I can drive you by the one I've been thinking about signing the dotted line on. That is, if you don't mind giving me your opinion."

"That would be fun." She sat up a little straighter in her seat and actually looked excited.

"I still have the code to the front door, so we can take a tour inside, too."

"Really? They let you walk around without someone being there?"

He laughed at her. "Remember, town sheriff here."

She smiled at him. "I almost forgot."

When he drove up the steep driveway, he was once again impressed by the place. The log cabin look had caught his eye right away. Tonight the front porch lights had been left on and the place seemed to glow.

The wide front porch looked inviting and he could just imagine himself sitting out there on a large swing, maybe watching a couple of dogs play in the front yard. The nearest neighbor was about a quarter of a mile down the road, but he didn't mind; he liked the solitude. The inside had recently been remodeled and it shined and looked brand new.

After parking in front of the oak garage doors, he walked around to open Amelia's door.

"Oh, I can't believe how lovely it is. I've never been up here before. I suppose there are other houses in town that I've never seen, but I can't believe I didn't know this one was here."

He followed her up onto the deck, but instead of going to the front door, she stood and looked out into the dark yard, leaning on the railing.

"I bet you can see the ocean from here." She turned and looked at him. He nodded his head in agreement.

"Yes, just through those trees there, but I had planned on trimming them down a bit so the view was unhindered."

"Wonderful. It's so far up here in the hills, too, yet still just two minutes to town."

He smiled. "Yes, that's why I think I chose it. And you should see the master bathroom." He walked to the door and entered the code in the keypad and tried the door. It opened quietly.

"Good, I remembered it correctly. Come on, I'll give you the tour."

She walked up to him and smiled. "Who used to live here?"

"Well, the last couple that lived here had moved to Pride from Portland two years ago. I guess they decided the slow life was too slow and moved back to the city. Before that, I'm not sure."

She walked into the entryway and he followed. There was a large sunken living room and the spacious kitchen was off the back to one side.

"It has four bedrooms and two-and-a-half baths. But the best part is the unfinished basement. Come check it out." He opened a door and they walked down the stairs together.

"I plan on building it out, maybe put in a large recreation room, a pool table, a large screen television, maybe even a built-in bar over there." He was caught up in the image; he could imagine it all.

"Robert, I think it's absolutely wonderful." She walked up and placed a soft kiss on his lips.

Seeing her walk to him in that dress did something to him, and he couldn't stop himself from pulling her back to him and resting his mouth tenderly on hers.

"Just one more." He rubbed his lips over her soft mouth and felt like he was on fire. Slowly he backed her up until she was against the wall as he continued to kiss her.

"Mmm, I can't believe you feel so good," he moaned into her neck as she grabbed him for support. Then she was pushing his jacket off his shoulders and running her hands over his arms. He held onto her hips and tried to fight the urge to rip the dress from her tight body. When she started undoing his buttons, he stopped her hands with his.

"Amelia, I don't … I can't…"

"Please, Robert, I want this." He'd imagined being with her a million times, but in an unfinished basement was not what he'd planned. Which didn't mean he couldn't enjoy her for a little while longer.

Running his hands up her arms, he cuffed her wrists with his hands and pulled them over her head against the wall. Her breasts pushed out towards him and he dipped his head to kiss a trail along the low line of her dress. Moving her wrists to one of his hands, he slowly pulled her dress down until she was exposed for his view. His hand traveled down the smooth line of her body as he licked his way from one breast to the other. When he reached the line of her skirt with his hand, he felt her soft skin and pushed the material up until she was exposed.

He ran his hand up the inside of her thigh and felt her quiver as he sucked lightly on her nipple. His fingers inched up until he cupped her through her silky panties. He could feel her getting wet in his hands and almost lost control. Her wrists were still cuffed above her head in his hand and he had no intention of letting her go. He wanted to be in control, he wanted to make her come.

Using his thumb, he pushed her panties aside and rubbed his fingers over the soft skin underneath. She bowed her back against the wall and gasped when he plunged a finger into her heat.

"Please, Robert," she moaned as he worked his fingers across her, enjoying the slick sounds of her excitement. He used his legs and knees to spread her legs wider, so she stood pinned against the wall, unable to do anything but enjoy his private torture.

He moved back up and took her mouth with his, enjoying her moans and gasps as he pleasured her. She tried to get out of his grip, so he moved a little closer and pinned her with his body, easily snuffing out her ability to touch him. He wouldn't be able to control himself if she touched him again, and he needed to be in control.

"Robert, I can't…"

"Go ahead, let go, no one will hear you. God! I want you so bad." He couldn't control himself; he dipped his head and took her nipple into his mouth again as she screamed out his name.

Chapter Six

The drive back to her house was a quiet one. She couldn't believe she'd just done that with him in someone else's home. When she looked over at him, she could tell he was still wound up. She felt bad, but he had told her he couldn't handle her touching him. Not yet.

She smiled again thinking that soon they had to arrange a time to be alone.

"When is your next day off?"

He looked at her and smiled. "Next Tuesday."

"Hmm, maybe I can plan our outing next time."

"You didn't like the dinner?" She watched his eyebrows crinkle.

"Oh, no! I loved it. I especially enjoyed seeing the house. I was just thinking about maybe doing something special for you."

"Amelia, you don't have to do anything special." He pulled into her mother's drive and when he cut the engine, he turned and looked at her and pulled her closer. "I just want to be with you." He kissed her again and she knew she couldn't get enough of him.

Finally she pulled back and smiled up at him. "I still want to plan something. Make sure you dress warm and bring a jacket. I'll pick you up around ten." She started to get out of the car.

"Wait," he reached for his door handle.

"No, you don't have to walk me to the door. Besides, if my mother answered, how would you explain that?" She smiled and nodded towards his crotch and the bulge in his pants.

He laughed. "Fair enough. Good night."

Amelia did everything she could to fill her time until she saw Robert again. She visited the Jordan's at the hospital, where Iian had woken a few days earlier. When she walked into the room to visit, Lacey had informed her of his condition.

"He's having some difficulty hearing. They're still running some tests, but it seems to be permanent." She could see the struggle in her friend's face. She sat with Lacey for a few hours while Iian rested. She remembered him as a scrawny kid who had always been underfoot when she had spent the night at her friends. But now his feet almost hung off the hospital bed. He still looked skinny and with all the injuries, he looked pale and weak.

After a few hours of visiting with Lacey, a tall man with curly blonde hair and wire-rimmed glasses came in with Todd.

"Amelia, this is Matthew Kimble. He's our neighbor and friend." She shook his hand and watched as he walked over to Iian's bed and wrote something on the notepad they were using to communicate with him. She quietly excused herself and hugged Lacey, promising she'd be back later in the week to visit again.

She had a few friends in Pride and had made a point to visit each of them, but felt closest to Lacey now, especially since they'd both just lost their fathers.

On the short drive home, she couldn't stop thinking about Robert and the anticipation for Tuesday would bubble up. When she hit the outskirts of town, she saw the lights behind her car and heard the siren. Smiling, she pulled over into a turnoff and stopped.

She watched him walk up to the car in her side mirror. When he walked up to her window, she couldn't stop thinking about getting him out of his uniform.

Jill Sanders

"Mrs. Blake." He nodded.

"Good evening, Sheriff. Is there anything in particular I can do for you today?" His smile was fast and potent. He cleared his throat and leaned down and kissed her right through her car window. She grabbed a hold of his hair and kept him there until she had had her fill of his mouth. She thought she heard a car horn honk at them, but she didn't care. She just enjoyed the feel of his hair in her hands and his lips on hers.

"You're going to get me fired if you keep that up." He braced his hands on her car door and leaned towards her. His smile was infectious.

"Is it Tuesday yet?" She smiled at him.

"I wish. I get off around ten tonight. Any chance you'll still be up? I can always swing by and we can neck on your front porch."

"I wish. I have an early interview tomorrow at the clinic. I think Tammy is going to hire me. She's been trying to move some things around in her budget to make room for me. I think she wants to see what I'm made of."

"Wow, that would be great. I know you'll get the job." He waved at another car that passed them.

"Damn, that was Mary. Now it will be all over town that we were talking."

"So, who cares? I don't mind people knowing that I'm dating the sheriff." When she said that, his smile got even wider.

"Really? Dating, huh?"

"Isn't that what you'd call this?" He thought about it and smiled again.

"Yeah, definitely dating."

"Good answer, Officer. I'd hate to have to get out of this car and kick your butt up and down Main Street."

He laughed. "Well, I better get back to patrolling," Another car whizzed by. "Give me a call if you have a free night. And let me know how the interview goes."

"Okay." She watched him walk back to his car and smiled when he honked two times and waited for her to pull out first.

Tuesday morning came and he waited for her car to pull up in front of the grocery store. He tried to catch her before she walked up the stairs outside in full view of everyone at the checkout counter, but she'd already made it halfway up when he met her.

"So, where are we going?" He asked.

"You'll see." She leaned up and kissed him as they reached her car. He knew that Patty's face would be plastered to the front windows. What the hell? he thought, then pulled her closer and deepened the kiss.

When she pulled away smiling at him, he said, "I thought I'd give the old girls something to gossip about."

"Well, I should think that would keep them entertained for a while. I know I have no complaints." He smiled at her and held her close and asked, "How did your interview go?"

"It went great. She is going to let me know in the next few days."

They drove a short ways to the pier and when she parked, he smiled. He'd always enjoyed going out on a boat. His aunt had never had one, so he didn't get to very often, though he did remember going out with Todd and his father once for a weekend trip.

"Do you have a boat?"

She nodded. "It's my father's. I'm thinking of selling it, but just haven't decided. I'm hoping by the end of the day I'll make up my mind."

"How good are you at being a captain?" He thought about it and tried not to show his worry.

"Don't worry, we won't go that far off shore." She took a small cooler from the trunk of her car. "Besides," she said as she looked over her shoulder at him, "I'm an excellent captain."

An hour later, he had to agree with her. She maneuvered the tiny vessel like she had been born on the water.

The weather was holding, and even though there was a chill in the air, the sun was still shining. She let him steer for a bit while she went below into the small cabin to prepare lunch. He enjoyed standing on the deck, watching the waves and the sky. He could get used to this. Maybe he'd try to save some money and buy one of these himself.

They sat on the deck and ate lunch while watching the sea lions play and sunbathe on the rocks near the shore. After eating, she leaned back against him and they watched the water.

"You know, I've had so much fun today, I don't want to go back."

"Then don't." She reached up and pulled his head down towards hers. He couldn't stop himself from taking the kiss deeper. He pulled her up into his lap as she ran her hands through his hair, over his shoulders, and down his chest.

"Amelia, you're trying to kill me, aren't you?" He pulled back, breathless and loving it.

"There is no need to be shy. I've learned that life is short and you need to grab what you want. And I want you, Robert."

"As long as you'll still think the same about me in the morning," he said as he pulled her back into a kiss. Then he was picking her up and trying to maneuver down the narrow stairs.

"Wait, I'd better walk down myself or we might end up hurting ourselves." She chuckled as he frowned at the small opening.

"I hope there's a bed down there." She laughed as he set her on her feet.

When he made it down the stairs behind her, he noticed a small kitchen area and in the back, to his relief, he saw a full size bed that took up the rest of the space. She turned towards him and wrapped her arms around his shoulders as she started kissing his neck and face. He walked her backwards towards the bed. When the back of her legs hit the thigh-high mattress, he stopped and pulled her close.

The gentle sway of the water and the way the light seeped into the cabin made for an almost surreal moment. He pulled back and just looked at her, her face in his hands. Her green eyes looked like emeralds and her hair shined amber, and he felt his heart take the leap he'd waited for all his life.

Amelia watched as Robert looked at her. She didn't know what he was thinking, why he was taking so long when she was on fire herself. How could he have such control over his desires? She had never felt the urgency that she was feeling now.

Arching up on her toes, she grabbed his hair and pulled him down to her mouth. His hands started moving over her, loosening buttons, pulling her clothes off. She pushed his shirt up and over his head and moaned when she saw the play of muscles there.

"You've been hiding this under that uniform? Mmmm, had I know this is what you looked like, I would have gotten you here a lot faster." She dipped her head and rained kisses along his collarbone. His skin stretched tight over a glorious display of pecs which rippled down to a complete and well-defined six-pack. She'd never seen a more awesome display of the male body than what was standing before her.

He pulled out a small foil package from his pocket and set it on the edge of the bed for later. Then he slowly removed her shirt, exposing the new panties she'd bought for just this occasion. She knew the deep red color was his favorite and was satisfied when she heard him moan with delight.

"You are so beautiful," he said as he looked at her. Then she was pulling his jeans down off his narrow hips, and she moaned when she saw the size of him. He was magnificent. She wanted to lick every inch of his body, but she lost track of her thoughts when he pulled her jeans off and knelt before her, kissing from her breasts down her stomach to just above her red panties. Her hands went to his hair to hold him there as he rolled his tongue around her navel. His fingers rubbed circles on her bottom, lightly stroking each cheek. Then he pulled her panties off and just looked at her.

"You are so beautiful," he repeated. His fingers ran lightly over her hips, edging towards her heat, until finally he ran his fingers over her. The feather light contact was almost too much for her to bear.

"Robert, I need you now, please." She pulled him down on the bed and started kissing him as she wrapped her legs around his hips, pressing their cores together.

"Amelia, god, how I need you." He kissed her, then quickly pulled back as he ripped open the condom package and sheathed himself, then slowly entered her.

She couldn't breathe. How could she feel so much from just his slow movements? Maybe it was the look in his dark eyes that told her she was in trouble. Maybe it was the sweet things he whispered in her ear as he slowly made love to her. Whatever it was, by the time his hips started pumping faster, she knew there was no way she'd get away without losing her heart.

Chapter Seven

They lay there holding each other until the light changed, and when she started to move to get up, he pulled her back down and started the slow dance again. He'd always imagined making love could be something he would feel down to his core, but had never experienced it until today.

He wondered if it was too soon to tell her how he felt. He wondered how she felt, if she felt the same way. Maybe he was crazy. After all, a person couldn't fall in love this quickly, right?

On the trip back to the docks, he couldn't stop thinking about it. He stood behind her and hugged her as she steered into port. The chilly wind was in their faces and the sun was sinking lower behind the clouds. It felt so good to hold her near and he hated for the day to end.

When they docked, Robert jumped out and tied the boat off.

"Listen, it's still early, how about you come over and we can have some dinner and watch a movie?" He helped her onto the dock and kept hold of her hand after she landed next to him.

"That sounds great."

He almost did another fist pump in excitement. When they pulled up in front of the store, he no longer cared who saw them together. He walked around and opened her door and pulled her into a deep kiss right there, for the whole town to see.

He supposed he was laying claim to her, telling everyone that she was his. He didn't care, it felt good holding her, and more importantly, it felt right.

Taking the stairs to his place, he was shocked to find his door slightly open.

"Hold on." He grabbed her arm and stopped her on the stairs.

"What is it?" She looked at him.

"My door's open. Head down to the store while I check it out." He moved closer to the door, wishing he had his weapon in hand.

"Robert? You can't go in there alone." She inched forward, trying to follow him.

"Amelia, please, just go downstairs. I'm sure it's nothing. I'll just check it out then come down and get you. Besides, maybe you can buy us some of Patty's rotisserie chicken for dinner while you're down there."

"Oh, okay. But if you're not down there in five minutes, we're coming up after you. And I know for a fact that Patty still has a shotgun under her counter."

He smiled and kissed her nose. He watched her go down the stairs and when he was satisfied that she had made it into the store, he turned back to his door. On closer examination, he could see that the handle had been broken.

Who would have done this? He looked around and saw plenty of people in the street. There is no way someone could have done this without being seen.

When he stepped in, his kitchen light was on and he could see the mess. His television was still there so he immediately crossed burglary off the list. He slowly walked down the hall towards his bedroom and noticed there was more destruction there. Nothing seemed to be stolen—his safe and his television were in their place—but everything was trashed. After he double-checked everything, he walked down to the store and spent the next twenty minutes talking to Patty and a group of people at the store. He'd assured them that they had nothing to worry about and hinted that it was most likely kids who'd broken in and just trashed his place.

Amelia helped him straighten up and after he'd fixed the front door lock, they sat down to eat. Whoever had broken in had shattered the last two plates he had, so they ate rotisserie chicken and potato salad on paper plates and drank cold beer as they watched an old movie.

After they ate, they sat on the couch and he tried to figure out how to get her to spend the night, though he knew she probably had to get home to her mother. But that didn't mean he couldn't enjoy his time with her. They were halfway through another movie, his arm resting across the back of the couch, when he pulled her closer, smiling as she snuggled into his chest. Leaning his head down, he started running kisses over her ear and down her neck. She moaned and angled her head, giving him better access.

She surprised him then by pulling away, but she quickly moved to straddle him. Her hips were in his hands, her mouth was on his, and he could have just stayed like that all night. But she started to move and he knew he didn't just want her for that night, he wanted her every night.

Their clothing hit the floor as their breathing quickened. He tried really hard to go slow like before, but her hands and mouth were everywhere. Before he knew it, she was sliding onto him and swaying her hips to an internal beat.

His eyes almost crossed when she started bouncing on his lap, her breasts in his face, her hair flowing around him, smelling of honeysuckle and the ocean.

He closed his eyes on a wave of desire, but it only caused him to feel what she was doing to him even more. Her soft skin surrounded him, engulfed him, possessed him. His fingers dug into her hips as he pushed her faster, harder. He heard her moan on her explosion and opened his eyes to watch her throw her head back during her climax.

More, he had to have more. Flipping positions, he knelt in front of her on the soft cushions and held her knees up to her chest as he pounded faster. She flung her arms over her head and held onto the side of the couch, closing her eyes tightly. Her hair was fanned out, looking like a ring of fire around her delicate face. Bending down, he took her mouth as he felt himself explode.

So the old saying was true. Even if the place were on fire, there was no way he could move from this spot. First off, he doubted he could see to get to the door. So far, everything was still white. His hearing had yet to return and his legs were still shaking. He'd never experienced anything quite like it. Her fingers ran up and down his back lightly, which happened to be the *only* thing he could feel at the moment.

He wanted to tell her how he felt, but in his vegetative state, he doubted he could put two words together.

With his face buried in her chest, he could feel it rise and fall. He could even hear the slight hum of her voice, but in his state, trying to figure out what the words were was just too much.

"Mmm, can't hear you. Wait until I get my senses back." He snuggled into her chest further.

He listened to her laugh and marveled at the sound and feel of it. Listening to her laugh made him think about her smile. She was the kind of woman who had a quick, flash smile. You know, the kind that when she smiles, you felt like you've just been given a quick peek at heaven. Its brightness usually had you thinking about it for the rest of the day.

He was so lost in his thoughts, that when she slapped his rear, he jumped, and she laughed some more.

"What? I'm up." He sat up and looked at her. She was still sprawled on his couch, but her eyes were full of laughter, something he enjoyed very much.

"I said, I had better get going. It's getting late."

He frowned, "Can't you just stay here? My bed's big enough."

She smiled at him. "I better not. My mother is expecting me back. Besides, I have to wait for the phone call from Tammy. She told me I'd know something by tomorrow. You could swing by for dinner, if you're free."

He frowned. "I have to work until midnight." He didn't like the fact that he couldn't find time to be with her. He wanted her to be there when he got home every night. He wanted to see her every morning. He watched her putting on her clothes and wished she didn't have to go.

"What's the frown for?" She waited until he sat next to her after slipping on his jeans.

"Time. It seems like we just don't have enough of it. I'm booked all weekend. I've got to train the new guys still and certify them, then I have a few personal matters I've got to deal with. I won't be free until Thursday next week, maybe even Friday." He pulled her closer, almost into his lap. "I want to be with you more. To be near you. Maybe we can meet for lunch?"

"What day?" She smiled as his hands ran over her shoulder and neck.

"Every day?"

She laughed and he frowned even more. When she noticed his face, she cleared her throat. "That sounds wonderful. If I get this job at the clinic, I don't know if I'll be able to get away every day, but I could try." He leaned over and kissed her again.

That next week was a busy one for him. He had to certify his new employees, he had a week's worth of paperwork that had piled up somehow, and he had to meet with his campaign manager for next year's election. People assured him he would win, and not just because he was the only qualified candidate. People actually believed in him and trusted him.

On top of all that, everyone wanted to talk to him about his break-in. People were concerned that someone had moved into town and was burglarizing people. The next town meeting was scheduled for just under a week and he planned on addressing any questions or issues they had then, but that didn't stop them from calling and interrupting his day.

Amelia called him the next day and told him she'd gotten the job at the veterinary clinic and would start that next week. He'd wanted to celebrate with her, but he was too booked. He promised her a rain check on the celebration.

Almost a week later, Iian Jordan was finally released from the hospital, so naturally everyone gathered at their place for the town's standard welcome home get-together.

He was excited; he'd called Amelia and they were going to attend the event together. It was their first official act as a couple. He had to say, it felt nice walking into a place full of his townspeople and seeing everyone smile at them and tell them how perfect they were for each other.

Iian sat in the corner and looked bored, like he'd rather be anywhere but there. Robert knew that they had hired a tutor to help teach them sign language. He'd planned on learning the basics sometime, if his schedule ever freed up. It was nice seeing everyone together, even if there was a dark cloud over the event, knowing that George Jordan would never return. The town had held a small service the week after the accident, and had placed a simple headstone near his wife's in the cemetery. Seeing how the family pulled together was nothing short of amazing. He hoped to have something like that someday. His aunt was always there for him, but he envied the closeness of siblings. When he thought about having his own family, he knew he wanted at least two kids.

When they finally left the gathering almost four hours later, they drove in silence. His mind was preoccupied with thinking about his future.

"Where are we going?" Amelia asked, turning towards him in the new truck he'd purchased in Edgeview earlier that week.

He smiled. "I have a surprise for you. Just sit back and enjoy the short trip. Oh, and when I tell you to, close your eyes, no peeking."

She crossed her arms over her chest and tried for a pout. "I never peek."

"Really?" He couldn't help but laugh. "Liar."

Another two minutes and he told her to close her eyes as he drove the rest of the way up the slanted driveway.

"Okay, open." He'd positioned it so his high beams hit the red ribbon he'd tied on the door.

When she opened her eyes, her brows crinkled and she frowned. "What's this all about?"

"I closed on it this morning. It's mine."

She clapped her hands and pulled him into a hug, all the while squealing her congratulations. "Oh, Robert! I can't believe it. That's so wonderful. When are you going to move in? I'm so happy for you!" It all came out as one long sentence.

"Well, come on in. I want you to get a proper look at the place. Last time we were here, well, let's just say we didn't get to see much." She laughed and almost jumped out of his truck.

"I don't have much to move in. I guess I need to go shopping for new furniture. I plan on moving my stuff in over the weekend."

He opened the door and motioned for her to walk in. She stepped in and stopped when she saw what he'd set up earlier that evening.

The table and chairs with the tall candles sat in the middle of the empty room. He walked over and flicked the lighter and got the candles glowing, then lit the wood and paper he had setup in the fireplace.

Last, he walked over and hit the button on the small radio and had soft music flowing in the empty room.

"When did you have time to do all this?" She walked into the room and straight to the flowers that sat on the fireplace, burying her face in them and breathing deeply.

"Just before lunch. I wanted to celebrate your new job in style. I know we ate a lot at the Jordan's, but I hope you saved room for dessert. I'll be right back." He walked towards the kitchen as she looked around the room.

When he stepped back in, she was still standing by the fireplace, watching him.

"Here, take a seat." He set the dish down and pulled out her chair. "I hope you like chocolate." He picked up the plate and set it in front of her.

They ate cake by candlelight and listened to soft music playing while they enjoyed each others company. Then he pulled out a soft blanket and laid it in front of the fireplace. He kissed her and pulled her down until he could run his hands over every inch of her. Then he ran his mouth over the same trails. She'd worn her green dress; it was one he'd seen before, but he couldn't get over how sexy she looked in it. It was low cut and the front crossed over itself. It was all tied together with a green belt, so that when he moved one side of the dress down, the other side fell open. Soon he had her breasts exposed for his viewing and tasting. He ran his mouth over every inch he'd exposed and continued downward, pulling her dress away as he went.

He rolled her stockings down her legs and kissed the path. He'd never tasted anything as good as the inside of her thighs.

"Robert," she moaned as he moved closer to the inside of her thigh.

"You taste so good." He used his fingers to pull the silk aside and enjoyed the softness of her skin underneath. Then he dipped his head and ran his tongue across her. She bucked under him and he played his hand over her while he lapped at her sweetness. He could drown in her taste, her sweet scent, her softness. She was moaning and making sexy little noises when he traveled back up and entered her slowly.

They made love for tow hours, before he took her home. He hated that she had to leave and realized as he drove her home that he knew what the next step he wanted to make was. So he could secure his and her future.

He was so preoccupied by his thoughts, he didn't see the man standing at the bottom of the dark stairs to his apartment until he spoke.

"Well, well, if it isn't little Robby. All grown up, I see."

Chapter Eight

The old saying goes that when you're mad you see red. Well, Robert could attest to that. Not only did his vision turn red, but he heard a loud buzzing in his head. He had Roy rammed up against the brick wall so fast he could see the instant fear in the older man's eyes.

"Roy, what the hell did you do with my mother?"

The man laughed and Robert could see he was missing half his teeth. The other half were black and almost rotted out of his mouth. He'd seen the footage in Vegas, so he knew Roy had lost weight and gotten older, but nothing could have prepared him for the crazy look in the man's eyes.

Instantly he could tell he was high. Most likely crack or heroine, if he had to guess. He was so grossed out by the stench coming off his clothes, he almost lost his hold on his shoulders.

"I didn't do nothing to your mama. She left on her own, I swear." He could tell the man was lying, he could see it in his eyes. "I just came here to check up on you. I heard you was looking for me in Vegas. Big shot cop-boy looking for me." Robert watched the man's eyes almost roll to the back of his head as he slurred his words together.

"That's it, you're going in my jail cell until I get straight answers from you." He started to pull the man up and figured he'd walk him the two blocks to the station if he had to. No way was he letting this man ride in his new truck, knowing he'd probably hurl in it the second he sat down.

"I ain't going nowhere with you. I just came to get some money. I figured you owed me after what I did." He flung his arms and Robert let go of him and watched as he teetered on his feet. Roy reached out and put his hand on the wall to steady himself.

"What the hell are you talking about?"

"I took care of you all that time. You owe me. I looked out for you like you was my own son."

Robert wanted to slam his fist into the man's face, but chose to grab his shirt front and start walking very quickly towards the station. Roy tried to fling his hand away, but Robert was not only in better shape, but sober.

Robert knew how to handle drunks and people who were high. You either talked them down, or you ignored them. Since Roy wasn't making any sense, he decided the latter was the best way for him not to kill the man where he stood.

Roy mumbled the entire two blocks, which took twice as long to walk as usual since Robert was practically dragging the man.

When he got there, he was too pissed to acknowledge his deputy who sat behind the counter waiting for the call to duty.

"Who's that?" Larry said, following him to the back. "We booking him on drunk driving?"

"No." Robert didn't even really acknowledge the kid.

"What are we booking him on? Do you want me to process him?" The town was small and usually the only people they had in the cell were the local drunks, sobering up for the night. But Larry's enthusiasm for booking someone new was almost laughable.

"This is Roy…" He pulled Roy around and looked at him in the face. "What's your last name?"

"Mc—McDonald." Robert raised his eyebrows, showing that he didn't believe the man.

"Roy McDonald?" Roy laughed when Robert said it.

"Eee-iii-eee-iii-oooo."

Robert pulled him up on his toes and growled at him. He ground his back teeth, trying to talk himself out of punching the man.

"What's your last name?" He shook the man.

Roy looked at him and Robert saw fear in the man's eyes again.

"Kenny, Roy Kenny."

"Larry, book and process Roy Kenny."

"On what charges?"

"Public nuisance and public intoxication. I don't want him to go anywhere until I get back in the morning. Do you hear me?"

"Yes, sir," Larry said as Robert dumped the man in the cell, then walked out.

Amelia walked into the station the next day around lunchtime and saw Robert sitting behind the desk. He didn't even look up when the bell chimed over the door.

"Busy?" She leaned against the counter and saw his eyes flash as he looked at her.

"Yes, but never too busy for you." He stood up and walked around and kissed her lightly on the lips. "What brings you here?"

"I heard from Patty that you've got a man locked up in here that you think might have something to do with your mother's disappearance."

"Man, word does travel fast around here."

She noticed that he looked like he hadn't slept all night.

"Why didn't you call me?"

He stopped and stared at her for almost a full minute. Then he blinked. "I – I was so caught up in being angry. I didn't think to call you."

She'd felt a little hurt when she'd heard Patty telling someone about what was going on. She'd almost felt betrayed, but now looking at his face, into his eyes, she could see he was so affected by the whole scenario, he hadn't thought about her.

"Robert..." She didn't care anymore, she was willing to take the jump even if she did get burned. "I want to be there for you. I want to be the one you call when you need someone to talk to. I'm tired of trying to sneak time with you at lunch. I know it's a little crazy, but I've known you forever, so it's not like we just met."

He smiled at her and pulled her closer. "Amelia, what are you saying?"

She pushed him back and almost laughed at his face. "You know what I'm trying to say."

He smiled even more. "Well, say it then." He pulled her back to him and waited.

"I can't believe that I've fallen in love with you so quickly. I don't know what I'm supposed to do next."

"I do. Marry me."

She wrapped her arms around his neck and went onto her toes and kissed him. "Of course, it's perfect." She laughed.

"Really? You'll really marry me?"

"Yes. Don't tell me that wasn't a real proposal. If it wasn't I may have to lock you up until you give me a real one."

He chuckled, "No, it was real. I just never imagined you'd say yes."

Just then one of his new deputies walked in and they broke apart until he smiled and walked into the back room.

"Well, I came over here to see if I could help." She straightened her shirt.

"Help with what?"

"I don't know. Just help."

You already have. I've been so angry since I saw him last night, I've been kind of in a daze. You're sunny face and smile have woken me up."

She looked at him and realized that what he was saying was true. The dark circles that had been under his eyes earlier were gone. The color in his face was back, and his eyes were shiny again. He actually looked like he'd had a full night's rest now. It was amazing how happiness could physically change him.

"Anytime, Sheriff, anytime."

"Forever." He leaned down and kissed her.

Two days later, he was nowhere near getting any answers from Roy. He'd even called in the state guys to see if they could question him. He had one last card up his sleeve and when he made the call to his buddy in New Mexico, he wondered if he was doing the right thing.

Eric was known for his questionable tactics for getting a confession out of someone. He'd never done anything illegal, but definitely questionable.

When he arrived in town, Robert almost wanted to call him off. But Eric assured him that everything would be okay. After all, Eric owed him a favor.

It had taken only three hours to get the confession from Roy. Eric walked out of the room, his head hung low, with a list of details Robert didn't want to know.

"Let me take care of this one for you, buddy," Eric said, keeping the information to himself. "I'll deal with the state and let you know what we find. He might be pulling a fast one on us. You never know with his kind. We'll check it out and let you know."

"No, I need to deal with it. I've lived with this question almost my whole life."

"Robert—" Just then the bell chimed and Amelia walked in. She looked between the men and rushed over to Robert's side.

"Is it bad?" she asked Eric, and when he nodded, she pulled Robert aside.

"Let him check it out. I'll stay with you tonight, at the house." He pulled her into a hug.

"I need to deal with this. I have to deal with this myself."

She pulled back and looked into his eyes. "Okay, but if you need me…"

He kissed her and held onto her for a minute more. "I should be back soon. It may take a couple days…"

She nodded her head. "Keep me posted."

It took just under a week. The information Roy had provided was sketchy. The old house he'd owned in the middle-of-nowhere New Mexico had burned to the ground three years back, right about the time he'd been spotted in Vegas.

It was on the fifth day there that they'd found his mother. She was wearing the yellow happy dress she'd worn to his birthday party, its dirty, faded colors a complete contrasts to what the little boy in him remembered.

His buddies at the New Mexico Police force tried to shield him, but he'd seen what he'd come to see. His mother hadn't abandoned him all those years ago. Knowing that her body had been in her car trunk that morning as he left for school made him even sadder. If he'd just looked. If he'd just told the cops that he'd seen her car there. So many other 'ifs' popped into his mind.

When he got back to the hotel that night, his phone was flashing with messages.

The first one was from Amelia, telling him that Eric had called her and explained what had happened. She said she'd booked the morning flight out of Portland and would be there around nine. He couldn't wait to see her, to hold her.

The next calls were from his deputies, telling him they had everything under control and to take his time coming back. He listened to his aunt cry and tell him how very sorry she was that he had to go through all this. Then there were over a dozen calls from several people in town: Father Michael, Patty O'Neil, Todd Jordan, and so many more.

In all his life, he'd never felt as loved as he had since he moved to Pride, except by his mother and father. He couldn't wait to get home and show everyone how much he cared for them in return.

Epilogue

"Run, Run!" Robert yelled, standing up and throwing his hands to the left. "Keep going!"

"Robert, would you sit back down? I think the whole town can hear you," Amelia chuckled.

"Everyone else is yelling, too." He smiled down at his wife's face, then turned just in time to see his son slide into home base. He screamed with joy as the whole team jumped up and down, and then a bunch of eight-year-olds rushed his son and engulfed him in a huge hug. If they were older, Robert had no doubt that they would have lifted him up on their shoulders. Todd and Megan Jordan sat beside them, his friend was being just as enthusiastic as he was as well as all the other men in the stands.

It had been almost ten years since that day in New Mexico when Amelia and he had buried his mother at the small cemetery. Ten years, and two kids later, and he showed no signs of slowing down in his effort to show the people of Pride how much he thought of them. Or how much he loved the woman sitting beside him.

He sat back down and pulled her into his lap and kissed her right there in front of his entire family.

All of a sudden, the cheers faded and there was only her.

If you've enjoyed this book, please consider leaving a review where you purchased it. Thanks! --Jill

Want a FREE copy of my Pride Series novella, Serving Pride? **Join my newsletter** *at* jillsanders.com *and get your copy today. You'll also be the first to hear about new releases, freebies, giveaways, and more.*

Follow Jill online at:
Web: www.jillsanders.com
Twitter: @jilllmsanders
Facebook: JillSandersBooks
Email: jill@jillsanders.com

Red Hot Christmas

Just in time for the holidays, take another wonderful trip to Oregon. Enjoy this sweet story about some new small-town people and learn about the lives and loves of a hot young couple. Don't miss this opportunity to catch up on some of your favorite book characters and the enchanting town of Pride.

Amber is new to Pride. As the new manager of the Golden Oar, she has big plans for helping make it one of the finest restaurants along the Oregon coast. But when she moves into town, she doesn't count on running into, and almost killing, the most gorgeous man she's ever laid eyes on.

Luke thinks he knows what he wants out of life. That is until the woman he's been waiting for all his life takes him down. Literally. Now he's out to prove he's not just another man-boy, but someone Amber can trust and come to love.

About the Author

Jill Sanders is the New York Times and USA Today bestselling author of the Pride Series, Secret Series and West Series romance novels. Having sold over 150,000 books within 6 months of her first release, she continues to lure new readers with her sweet and sexy stories. Her books are available in every English speaking country and are now being translated to 6 different languages, and recorded for audiobook.

Born as an identical twin to a large family, she was raised in the Pacific Northwest, later relocating to Colorado for college and a successful IT career before discovering her talent as a writer. She now makes her home in charming rural Texas where she enjoys hiking, swimming, wine-tasting, and of course writing.

11044787R10057

Made in the USA
Lexington, KY
09 October 2018